The Mysterious Moortown Bridge

Weekly Reader Books presents

The Mysterious Moortown Bridge

LYNN HALL

Illustrated by Ruth Sanderson

Designed by Karen A. Yops

Library of Congress Cataloging in Publication Data

Hall, Lynn.
  The mysterious Moortown bridge.

  SUMMARY: While on a camping trip with their families,
Curtis and Pat discover a ghost town in a heavily wooded
ravine.
  [1. Mystery and detective stories]   I. Sanderson,
Ruth.   II. Title.
PZ7.H1458Mw   [Fic]   80–18808
ISBN 0–695–41468–2

Second Printing

Chapter 1

The sun rose above the trees that crowned the ridge, sending golden shafts of light down into the valley. The rays touched the roof of the Circle M Campground store and reflected brightly from the trailers and pickup campers parked among the trees.

It was October in northern Iowa, and the grass beneath the trees was white with last night's frost. Pat felt the crispness of it through her shoes when she jumped down from the door of her family's pickup camper. The frosty grass felt good to her. Everything felt good this morning. She loved the bright, clear sky and the reds and golds of

7

the trees on the surrounding hillsides. She smiled as she thought of the horses waiting for her in the corral behind the camp store.

Her parents were still asleep in the camper. Pat had fixed her own breakfast of milk and doughnuts from the camper's tiny refrigerator. Now she was ready to ride. She looked around for Curtis and saw him coming out of the shower building.

Curtis Wells was one of Pat's favorite friends, even though they saw each other only once a year, on this camping weekend

at Circle M. Pat's family lived in Des Moines, and Curtis's in Chicago. Last night, while their parents played cards and laughed at jokes Pat seldom understood, she and Curtis had made plans for today. They wanted to ride all day, if possible, and without a trail guide.

They found Mr. Martin, the campground owner, in the store, which was also an office, souvenir shop, and recreation room. He was making coffee in a huge pot.

"You two are up early," he said.

"We want to go riding. Could we go alone?" Pat asked.

"Well, I 'spect you could, as long as it's okay with your folks. You both know how to ride."

They went out to the corral, and Mr. Martin saddled two small, quiet horses. Pat climbed atop a black horse named Barney, and Curtis mounted Nugget, a creamy palomino.

"If you get lost," Mr. Martin said, "just give the horses their heads, and they'll bring you home. No galloping, and stay on the trails. And bring them back by lunch-time, you hear?"

"We will," Pat and Curtis called.

Smiling, Pat settled into the feel and the rhythm of Barney's movement. The trail led along the valley floor, among trees that were shedding a gentle brown rain of leaves. After a while the two riders left the main trail and followed a smaller one that climbed the valley wall. Limestone boulders jutted out along the way. Pat began to feel pleasantly unreal, as though she were a character in a western movie. There should be music in the background, she thought, grinning to herself.

"Have you ever been up here?" Curtis asked.

"No. Have you?"

"No. Let's see if we can go up higher."

Their trail was now running along the hillside, rather than climbing it. On the left they could look down at the valley floor, where the woods gradually thinned to open pasture. On the right the hillside rose, steep and rock-strewn.

"There's a path," Curtis called, pointing. "Let's see where that one goes."

It wasn't much of a trail, and it rose quite steeply, but Pat didn't want Curtis to think she was afraid. With a firm grip on her saddle horn, she reined Barney onto the narrow track.

It was a hard, scrambling climb for several minutes. Then it leveled out, so the riding was easy again. The woods were close around them now. They came over the top of the hill. Below them lay another valley, smaller and more darkly wooded than the Circle M valley.

"Look," Pat said suddenly. "Isn't that a road down there? Do you see it?"

Curtis nodded.

Far below, a road had been carved out of the hillside. It was narrow and grass grown and almost hidden by the trees. In wordless agreement, Pat and Curtis began angling their horses down the steep face of the valley wall. After a few scares, a few slides, and a near-fall, they reached the road.

"Boy," Curtis said, "nobody's been back here in a long time."

The valley was dark, and an odd, eerie feeling hung in the air. Wild grapevines grew everywhere, covering tree trunks and trailing from limbs. It seemed to Pat that the birds were quieter here. She got goose bumps on her arms.

They followed the road downhill, around curves, and sometimes through thickets of wild raspberry. A small river appeared on their right and followed the road.

Pat's horse stopped suddenly.

Ahead, through the trees, was a building. It looked like a long, narrow shed, straddling the river. Moss covered its shingled roof, and daylight showed through the broken boards of its sides.

"Hey, look at that," Pat said. "It's a covered bridge, isn't it? I've seen pictures of them, but I never saw a real one before. And look over there!"

Beyond the bridge, on the far bank of

the river, stood a mill and a handful of small, rotting buildings. There were some houses, a store, and a structure that might have been a warehouse. The mill was built of cream-colored stones cut in huge blocks. It stood straight and clean and was reflected straight and clean in the river water. The other buildings were caving in. Some were covered with grapevines.

Again, Pat felt goose bumps rise on her skin.

"Come on. Let's go explore!" Curtis whooped.

Pat urged Barney toward the bridge, but the horse grew tense. His ears moved back and forth, as though he were listening to sounds Pat couldn't hear. His nostrils widened, and his eyes showed white rims of fear. He planted his feet and refused to move.

"See if you can get Nugget across the bridge," Pat called. Her jaw was clenched in her effort to force Barney forward.

Nugget was no better. He whirled, half-rearing, and stared into the black tunnel of the bridge as though it contained an invisible monster.

Pat got off and tried to lead Barney onto

the bridge. He snorted and jerked back so hard that he tore the reins out of her hand. He spun and galloped away, cracking into Nugget as he turned. The jolt nearly knocked Curtis from his saddle.

Suddenly there was a laugh, high and wild.

A figure stood in the darkness of the old covered bridge. It was silhouetted against the sunlight beyond. The shape was small, bent—an old woman.

Her voice came echoing from the hollow of the bridge.

"Foolish children! Trying to make your horses cross Moortown bridge. Don't you *know?*" Again the laughter rang crazily around them. The sound struck like a pain in Pat's head.

"Let's get out of here!" Curtis yelled.

Pat scrambled up onto Nugget behind Curtis, and they rode away on the fear-sweated animal.

Chapter 2

Not far down the road they caught up with Barney. He had stopped running and was grazing with quick, nervous bites. His eyes still had a wild, scared look to them, but he allowed Pat to catch him and climb into the saddle.

As they rode up the steep hillside, Pat felt both relief and regret. The dark, narrow valley was somehow frightening, with its vine-draped trees and crazy woman, or whatever she was. And yet, as Pat looked back from the crest of the hill, her curiosity tugged at her. She felt herself wanting to go back, to find out more about the place.

Pat and Curtis wove among the trees and

17

boulders down into the Circle M valley. When they were safely back on the trail, Curtis let out a long-held breath.

"That was a scary place. You know what that was, Pat? It was a ghost town. Only I never knew they had ghost towns around here. I thought they were just out west."

Pat hugged her elbows to her sides to hold in a shiver. "It was a ghost town, all right. Complete with ghost."

"Oh, she wasn't a ghost." Curtis laughed nervously. "She was a witch. She bewitched the horses so they wouldn't go across her bridge."

"That's stupid, Curtis. She wasn't a ghost or a witch. Just an old lady. Probably crazy as a bedbug, though."

They reached the valley floor, where the trail was wide enough to ride side by side. Hereford cattle raised their white heads and watched the riders pass. Squirrels raced in the tree limbs, their cheeks fat with acorns. Now that the ride was almost over, Pat wanted it to go on and on. This crisp, sunny October Saturday was a jewel of a day. She didn't want to waste it hanging around the campground all afternoon with her parents.

Curtis felt the same way. "You know what we should do?" he said. "We should go camping tonight."

Pat gave him a sideways look. "What do you mean? We *are* camping."

"No, I don't mean in the campers with our parents. I mean just you and me, out in the woods. I know Mr. Martin has backpack tents and sleeping bags that he rents out. We could take food along. Let's see if they'll let us."

Pat's eyes began to sparkle. "It'd be fun," she said. Then she shook her head. "But they probably wouldn't let us. They'd say it's too cold. My parents would, anyway."

"Maybe not," Curtis insisted. "I've been on Scout camp-outs in lots colder weather than this. And there isn't anything dangerous about it. There aren't any bears or wildcats around here, nothing like that. We could go back there." He motioned with his head toward the ghost town, now hidden behind the hill.

Pat felt a chill of fearful excitement. She thought, To spend a long dark night in that valley . . .

Curtis was watching her expression. "Scaredy-cat," he teased.

19

"I am not! I just don't think my parents will let me, that's all."

"Let's try, anyhow," Curtis urged.

"Okay. Sure. It'd be fun."

When they got back to the campground, they hauled the heavy saddles off Barney and Nugget. Then they hung the saddles and bridles on the fence and turned the horses loose in the corral.

"We'll be back for you later, if we're lucky," Pat told Barney.

Pat and Curtis left each other to go in search of their parents. Pat's camper was locked, but taped to the door was an envelope with a message written on it.

"Patsy, we've all gone fishing. Be gone most of the day. If you want us, Mr. Martin can show you where we are. Here's some lunch money. Love, Mom."

Inside the envelope was a dollar. Pat stuffed it into her pocket and headed for the store. She was painfully hungry all of a sudden. On the way she met Curtis coming from his trailer. He, too, had lunch money and a note. They decided to eat first and then find their families.

Mr. Martin was in the store. "I see you got back safe and sound from your ride," he said. "Your folks just went off fishing a

little bit ago. Upstream a ways."

"I know," Pat said. "They left us lunch money. I want a Chuck Wagon Delight and a Coke, please."

"Me, too," Curtis said.

While the fat Chuck Wagon sandwiches were being heated in the microwave oven, Pat opened her Coke and took a long, lovely drink.

"Where did you kids ride to?" Mr. Martin asked pleasantly.

Curtis and Pat glanced at each other, wondering if it would be safe to tell him. Would he be angry that they had gone into the next valley, riding the horses up over that steep slope?

But Pat had already learned that she usually got into far less trouble when she was honest with adults than she did when she tried to cover something up. It seemed to her that grown-ups could always tell, somehow. Besides, she was terribly curious about the ghost town. She wanted to find out what Mr. Martin knew about it.

"We went back to where that covered bridge is, and those empty houses," she said. "What is that place, anyway? It was spooky."

Mr. Martin laughed, and Pat and Curtis

relaxed. He wasn't mad after all. "That's Moortown—and the old Moortown bridge. Yes, I'd say 'spooky' is a good way to describe it."

"Is it a ghost town?" Curtis asked.

"Oh, you could call it that, I suppose. It never did get to be much of a place. The mill went out of business about as soon as it was started. The same with the store."

"But why?" Pat asked.

Just then the microwave oven timer dinged, and Mr. Martin pulled out the steaming sandwiches in their wrappers.

He scratched his beard. "Well, now, there used to be some funny stories about that place. But you know how people talk. Couldn't have been anything to it."

He turned away, toward the back room of the store.

"Wait," Pat called between gulps of her sandwich. "Please. Tell us the rest, Mr. Martin. What kind of stories?"

Mr. Martin looked as though he felt a little foolish. "Oh, you know. Somebody starts talking about a ghost, and the first thing you know, people start calling a place 'haunted,' and it's all a lot of nonsense."

"What was haunted?" Pat asked eagerly. "One of the houses?"

He shook his head. "The bridge."

Pat and Curtis stared at him, then at each other, forgetting to chew.

Curtis swallowed. "Why do people think it's haunted?"

Mr. Martin shrugged. "Like I said, it's all nonsense. Only I guess the mill and store went out of business because people couldn't get their teams to pull their wagons across the bridge. That was back in the days before cars, of course. The farmers would haul their grain to the mill to have it ground into flour. That is, they tried to, but the horses just didn't seem to like that bridge for some reason. At least, that's the way I heard the story."

Pat looked at Curtis. She was thinking about Barney and Nugget. They had refused to cross the bridge, too. Curtis was thinking the same thing. Pat could see it in his eyes.

"Funny thing," Mr. Martin said thoughtfully, scratching his beard again.

"What?" Pat and Curtis asked together.

"It was just a coincidence." Mr. Martin laughed a little. "Several years ago the Clayton County Tourism Committee—"

"What's that?" Curtis interrupted.

"The Tourism Committee? Oh, that's a

bunch of people trying to make this county a good place for other people to come on vacations. As I started to say, the committee decided to try to restore Moortown, as a tourist attraction. It's got the only covered bridge in this part of the state, and the mill's a beautiful old building. Well, a few of us drove down there one day to take a look at it. The road was in better shape then. You could get back there from the county road."

"What happened?" Pat prodded. She wished he'd get to the good part.

Mr. Martin looked embarrassed, as though afraid of sounding silly. "The car stalled. We'd just started across the bridge, and the darned thing died. We got it started again, but the other committee members decided they didn't want to drive across, after all. They got to talking about the old stories, about the bridge being haunted and all that nonsense. We backed the car off the bridge, parked it, and walked over for a look around. But some of the committee people were pretty nervous about the whole thing. And when it came time to vote on the project at the next meeting, they voted not to try to make Moortown a tourist attraction after all."

Chapter 3

"There they are," Pat said, pointing to a spot across the pasture. She could see her father and mother with Curtis's parents, and one or two other campers. They were fishing along the bank of the trout stream that wound along the valley floor.

Pat and Curtis ran toward them. As the two approached, Pat's father looked up and signaled for them to be quiet.

"Don't scare away the fish," he said.

Pat's mother laughed. "I think the fish were scared away from here a long time ago. I haven't even had a nibble all this time. Hi, Sugar. Did you have a nice ride this morning? Did you get some lunch?"

27

Pat had to catch her breath from running. "We had Chuck Wagon Delights at the store." She paused for a moment and then asked, "Mom, could me and Curtis go camping by ourselves tonight?"

"Curtis and I," Mrs. Hines corrected. "Camping by yourselves? I don't know. Where were you going to go?"

Pat's father and Curtis's parents were drawn into the conversation.

Curtis explained, "We found a neat place while we were riding this morning, and we want to go back there. We asked Mr. Martin if he'd rent us the horses again. And he has bedrolls that he rents. He said people go on two-day trail rides here sometimes, so he has these little one-person tents and sleeping bags. They roll up and tie on the back of a saddle. He said we couldn't have a campfire because we might burn down the woods. But other than that, he said there wasn't any reason we couldn't manage by ourselves—if we got your permission. Please? Just think. That'll get us out of your hair clear till tomorrow morning. Wouldn't it be nice to be rid of us that long?"

All four parents laughed, and Pat and

Curtis grinned at each other. The battle was won.

It was nearly dark by the time Pat and Curtis caught sight of the Moortown bridge. "Where shall we camp?" Pat asked. She thought, Let's not go any closer, but she didn't say it out loud.

They tied the horses and explored a little on foot. Near the bank of the river they found a small, grassy clearing that looked like a good spot. They could see the bridge, and the mill beyond the river. But the trees and bushes around them gave Pat a feeling of concealment, of being safely hidden from—whoever might be watching.

They left the horses on long halter ropes to graze. Then Pat and Curtis unsaddled and began unfolding the tents. The blue nylon tents were very small, each just big enough to hold one sleeping bag. While Curtis worked at setting up the tents, Pat carried river water to Barney and Nugget. The horses were already getting wound up in each other's ropes. By the time Pat got them straightened out, Curtis had both tents up.

"Let's go see the bridge," Curtis said

eagerly. "Or do you think it's too late?"
They looked around at the darkening valley.

With some relief Pat said, "I guess we'll
have to wait till morning. Let's have sup-
per now."

Grinning, the two sat cross-legged on the
ground and unpacked the meal they had
brought: cold fried chicken, baked beans,
carrot sticks, and hot chocolate from a
thermos bottle. Everything was delicious.

Pat's mind was on the rest of the camp-
out. This is going to be a real adventure, she
thought. Years from now, when I'm old, I
bet I'll still remember it and talk about it.

There was just enough fear and mystery in the outing to make it seem exciting.

Curtis waved toward the black shapes of the buildings across the river. "Do you suppose *she* lives over there?"

"She? You mean the ghost, or witch, or whatever she is?"

"Yes," Curtis said, in the kind of voice people use when telling ghost stories. "Maybe we should have brought a wooden stake to drive through her heart."

Pat tossed a chicken bone at him. "You dummy. That's for killing vampires, not ghosts or witches. Ghosts can't be killed.

They're already dead. And I think for witches you just give them the evil eye, or sprinkle garlic on them, or something."

Curtis continued, "What if—Pat, look!" He grabbed her arm.

Across the river, near the mill, something moved. It looked like the same figure they had seen, laughing, on the bridge that morning. The small figure moved slowly along the riverbank toward the bridge, her shapeless garments blowing in the night breeze.

Curtis's hand tightened on Pat's arm. Pat thought she heard the woman's voice, high and frail and soft, across the moon-sparkled water. The woman seemed to be talking to herself.

"What if she comes over here?" Curtis whispered nervously.

"She won't. I bet she won't cross the bridge." Pat didn't really believe her own words, but they sounded reassuring.

The figure came to the bridge. She stepped onto it and disappeared from sight behind its walls.

"She's coming across!" Curtis squeaked.

Suddenly they saw a tiny dot of light on the steep hillside behind the Moortown buildings. It moved and bobbed slowly down toward the valley.

Pat could scarcely breathe.

In the distance a woman's voice called, strong and clear, "Aunt Evvie, Aunt Evvie."

The little figure emerged from the bridge and shuffled back toward the mill and the descending dot of light.

"It's just a flashlight," Curtis said, feeling foolish at the scare they had given themselves.

The dot of light and the shuffling figure both disappeared behind the mill. In a few minutes the light began to climb the hill again, this time with Aunt Evvie in tow, Pat supposed.

Suddenly she and Curtis were breathing again and laughing at themselves.

"She's not a witch *or* a ghost," Pat said. "Just somebody's weird aunt who goes wandering around at night. There must be a house on top of that hill someplace."

They talked until they were too sleepy to talk any longer. Then they crawled into their tents and zipped themselves into their sleeping bags.

But sleep didn't come for Pat. The night sounds were too near, too loud. At home she could sleep through almost any noise, but here the soft rustlings in the woods kept her rigid and wide-eyed far into the night.

Finally she slept. During the night she thought she heard laughter, far away and high and wild. When she woke up, she was almost sure she'd been dreaming.

Almost.

Chapter 4

Pat crawled out of her sleeping bag and unzipped the door of her tent. The sky was bright blue, but the sun had not yet reached down into the narrow valley. Blue shadows lay over the clearing, the river, and the buildings beyond.

Pat could see her breath, silver puffs that came and went. She felt she needed a bath after sleeping in her jeans and sweat shirt all night. But the air was too cold even to think about washing in the river.

Curtis approached from the direction of the horses.

"I thought you were never going to wake up," he grumbled.

"Are the horses okay?"

"Sure. All tangled up in their ropes, but I got them straightened out, and I gave them some more water. Let's hurry up and eat breakfast, so we can go explore."

Breakfast was doughnuts and orange juice in little cartons from the camp store. It didn't take long to eat. Pat stood up, brushed the crumbs from her sweat shirt, and said, "Okay, let's go."

They ran along the riverbank until they were close to the bridge. Slowly, they approached the wooden structure. The sun was above the rim of the valley now, melting away the shadows and gilding the river. Without the fright of the horses, there seemed to be nothing spooky about the bridge this morning.

Still, Pat and Curtis moved a little closer to each other as they stepped onto the bridge. It was like entering a dark tunnel. A sudden noise near Pat's head made her jump. But it was just a bird. Pat looked up and saw several nests along the roof beams.

From the inside the bridge didn't seem as dark a tunnel as it had at first, Pat realized. Several large holes in the roof let in beams of sunlight, and many of the side boards were gone. Near the middle of the bridge was a very large hole in one side.

"Curtis, look at that hole. It looks as though—oh!" Suddenly Pat's toe caught, and she fell flat.

"Did you hurt yourself?" Curtis asked. He tried not to give in to the usual urge to laugh when someone falls. But he ended up laughing anyway. It broke the tension in the air.

Pat sat up and rubbed one knee. "No, just fell over my feet. I'm so graceful."

Curtis bent over the plank flooring and ran his fingers along the rough wood. "Look here, Pat. This is what you tripped over."

A chunk of plank had split and pulled away from the flooring slightly. It was just high enough to catch Pat's shoe.

"What about it?" she said. "This bridge is probably a hundred years old. What's so surprising about a hunk breaking off?"

"These," Curtis said with growing excitement. "Look closer."

On hands and knees Pat and Curtis examined the floor plank. There were holes in it, small, neat round holes, a cluster of

them on the split board and a scattering in other places.

"What could have made them?" Pat wondered aloud. Abruptly, she sat back and stared at Curtis. He was looking at her the same way, as though an amazing thought had just occurred.

"Have I been watching too much television," Curtis said slowly, "or do these look like bullet holes to you, too?"

"That's just what I was going to say. Is this what bullet holes look like?"

"How should I know? I guess so," Curtis said. "Look. They go straight through the wood, not at an angle. So whoever was shooting must have stood right here and fired down at the floor of the bridge. Why, I wonder."

Pat studied the split board. "Or," she said slowly, "the person could have been standing *under* the bridge, firing up through the floor. It looks as if that splintered-off hunk was pushed *up*, doesn't it?"

They stared at each other again. Then, together, they scrambled to the side of the bridge where the wall was broken away. They looked down.

The river was not far below. It was shallow and sandy-bottomed, but strewn with large rocks that appeared to have rolled down from the hillsides.

"Well," said Curtis, "it looks as if someone could have waded in under the bridge and shot a gun up through the floor, like you said. But why?"

Pat looked up and around. She and Curtis were framed in a hole several feet wide that reached from floor to roof.

"What do you think made this hole?" she asked.

Curtis glanced at it. "It probably rotted away. Lots of the boards are missing."

"Yes, but not—" A sudden movement had caught Pat's attention. "Here comes Aunt Evvie," she whispered.

Through the end of the bridge they could see the little figure approaching. She stopped to pick something from the roadside near the mill. Then she came on toward the bridge, chattering to herself.

"Let's talk to her," Pat said. Somehow, knowing the old woman's name was Aunt Evvie made Pat no longer afraid of her. "After all, what's an Aunt Evvie going to do to us?" she reasoned aloud.

The woman stopped just outside the bridge. "Good morning, children," she said.

Her voice was high and thin, but not really scary, Pat told herself.

"Good morning," Pat and Curtis answered.

"You children shouldn't play on his bridge, you know," Aunt Evvie said. "He wouldn't like it."

"Who?" Pat asked.

"Why, *him*, of course." Aunt Evvie motioned toward the air between her and Pat.

Crazy as a bedbug, Pat thought. She began walking toward the woman, with Curtis right behind. At closer range the woman didn't seem out of the ordinary, except that she was obviously extremely old. Her face was a mask of wrinkles, and her shiny scalp showed through her thin white hair. Her dress was black and old-fashioned, but not too strange.

"We were interested in the bridge," Pat said politely. "Could you tell us—"

"Look out!" the woman screamed.

Pat stopped. Curtis bumped into her. Heart pounding, Pat looked around. She could see no danger.

"You walked right into him," Aunt Evvie shrilled. She sounded furious. "Don't you young people have any respect for anything? You walked right into him." She

turned and hobbled away, amazingly fast. She was weeping.

Wide-eyed and silent, Pat and Curtis moved to follow Aunt Evvie. But they walked well around the spot in the middle of the bridge entrance where "he" was.

Chapter 5

They caught up with Aunt Evvie near the mill. She had stopped crying, but she still looked childishly resentful. In her hands, clutched to her chest, she held a milkweed. Its silvery-gray pod had exploded, and spun-silver fluff swirled in the air.

"We're sorry," Pat said. "We didn't mean to run into—him. Could you tell us who 'he' is?"

"As if you didn't know," the old woman snapped.

"But we don't," Curtis said. "We don't live around here. We're just here for the weekend, at the Circle M."

Aunt Evvie drew herself up straight. She spoke in a haughty tone. "I don't know what a Circle M is, but whatever it is, you should go back there. This is my valley. Isn't it, Ruth?"

Pat jumped and looked around. Standing behind her was another woman, a large middle-aged woman with a quiet face. She smiled at Pat and Curtis, then moved toward the old woman.

"Aunt Evvie, you have to get ready for church now. You go on home, dear, and I'll have a word with these young people."

Aunt Evvie jabbed at Pat with the milkweed, startling her. "They're bad children. Don't talk to them."

"I'm sure they're not bad," Ruth said, sending a small, warm smile toward Pat and Curtis. Her expression seemed to say, "Don't mind Aunt Evvie."

The old woman whined, "Yes, they are bad. I told them to stop, and they walked right into him. That wasn't nice."

Ruth soothed and patted the old woman. "You're right, dear. That wasn't very nice of them. You go along up the hill now. I'll scold the children, so they won't do it again. Maybe you can find some more

45

milkweeds, and we'll make a decoration out of them after church. Go along now."

Aunt Evvie turned and shuffled away, talking to herself. She began to climb a path that led up the steep hillside behind the mill.

Ruth turned to Pat and Curtis. "You mustn't mind what she says. Aunt Evvie is very old. She's ninety-seven, and her mind is pretty well gone by now."

The three of them watched the little figure make her way up the hillside.

Pat said, "She certainly gets around well for her age, though. We saw her down here yesterday morning and again last night."

Ruth looked at her curiously, so Pat explained. "Our folks are camping at the Circle M Campground, and we rode over here yesterday on horseback. Then we came back and camped overnight by ourselves. You can see our tents." She waved toward the patches of bright blue across the river.

Ruth's eyes twinkled. "Then you're pretty brave youngsters. Or didn't you know this place is supposed to be haunted?"

"Oh, tell us about it, please." Curtis said eagerly. "We were exploring the bridge, and it looked as if it had bullet holes in the bottom of it. And our horses wouldn't go across, and Mr. Martin was telling us something about the bridge being haunted—"

"And who the dickens is 'he'?" Pat asked.

Ruth cocked her head to one side and looked from Pat to Curtis, as though she were deciding whether they could be trusted with the truth. Then she looked at her watch.

"I guess I've got a little time before church," she said finally. "Here, let's sit down."

She went to the wall of the mill. The window openings in the thick stone wall made excellent sitting places. Ruth and Pat sat in a window, leaning against its sides, while Curtis dropped to the grass.

Ruth looked up toward Aunt Evvie's receding form, and the others did, too. It seemed as though Ruth was looking for a way to begin.

Pat broke the silence. "Is she really your aunt?"

Ruth shook her head. "She's my husband's great-aunt, matter of fact. That's our farm, up there, the back part of it. The house is quite a ways farther. I try to keep my eye on Evvie, but every chance she gets, she slips away from me and comes down here."

"Like a little kid," Pat said without thinking.

"Yes." Ruth smiled. "She is very much like a child now. She always has been a little, well, confused in the head. But it's gotten more noticeable as she's grown older."

Curtis said, "Why does she come down here all the time? Does it have something to do with the bridge?"

"And who is 'he'?" Pat asked again.

"It's a long story, but if you want to hear it, I'll tell it to you." Ruth made herself comfortable against the stone walls of the mill and then began her story.

Chapter 6

In the early 1880s a man named Joseph
Moor came to a tiny wooded valley in the
northeast part of Iowa. He had come all
the way from Scotland, hoping to make a
life for himself in the sparsely settled mid-
lands of America. But the bigness and open-
ness of the land made him feel uneasy. His
home in Scotland had been in the moun-
tains, and that was the kind of land that
felt right to him.

When he found the little valley, it re-
minded him of his old home, and he decided that this was going to be his place.
No one else had staked a claim on it. It
was too hard to reach.

Mr. Moor built himself a little house, and then he hired two stonemasons to build him a mill, so he could make his living grinding grain for the farmers in the area. The house and mill were built on the west bank of the river in a small area of flat land.

Then Mr. Moor hired a road crew to clear a road into the valley. Cliffs jutted out all the way to the river on the west bank, above and below the mill, so the road had to go on the east side. That meant there would have to be a bridge. Mr. Moor and the road crew could ride through the shallow water easily enough on their horses, but farmers hauling wagons of grain would need a bridge.

Mr. Moor found a local man, Charlie Slater, who had done some bridge building. He told Charlie how he wanted the bridge to be built—twelve feet wide, and solid, and covered with a sturdy roof. For building the bridge, Mr. Moor would pay Charlie and his helpers three hundred dollars.

The men shook hands, and Charlie went to work. He and his brother and a neighbor worked most of the summer, neglecting their crops in order to finish the bridge by fall. Having a mill so close to home would save all of them a two-day drive to McGregor each harvest season, so they were eager to complete the bridge. Also, that three hundred dollars would have to feed their families through the coming winter.

By early fall the bridge was complete. Charlie went to Mr. Moor to ask for his money. But when Mr. Moor gave the bridge his final inspection, he shook his head.

"It's not what we agreed on, Slater. I said twelve feet wide, and it's not." Moor pulled out a measure and checked the distance between the corner posts of the bridge frame. Eleven feet, two inches.

Charlie swore, grabbed the measure, and measured to the outside edge of the bridge, rather than just the distance between the corner posts. Twelve feet, plus a little.

"There's your twelve feet, you dangblasted fool," Charlie shouted.

But Mr. Moor pressed his lips together and shook his head. "It's not the outside measure that counts; it's the inside. That's where the wagons have to get through. I'll pay you one hundred dollars to cover the cost of materials, but not a penny more."

Charlie exploded. He raged. He shook Mr. Moor by the lapels and drew back to punch the Scotsman in the face, but his brother stopped him. Charlie argued and cursed and threatened, but Mr. Moor's mind was made up.

As his brother hauled him away, Charlie yelled, "All right, Moor. You got your bridge, but it'll be a cold day in July before anyone crosses it. I'll ruin your business. Nobody cheats Charlie Slater and gets away with it!"

Starting the next day, Charlie Slater sat in the middle of the bridge with his weapons—a tree branch tied with rags and bits of metal, and an old tin wash pan. Whenever a team approached the bridge, Charlie leaped toward the horses, waving his branch and banging the wash pan against the wall of the bridge. Horses shied, backed away, and sometimes turned and bolted.

After a few days Mr. Moor brought the sheriff, who told Charlie he was not to set foot on the Moortown bridge. Ever.

The next day Charlie took up a new position, on a large rock in the middle of the river, directly under the bridge. From there he proceeded to frighten every approaching horse. He banged on the floor planks with a long pole, and if that didn't work, he fired his gun. Sometimes he aimed out to the side of the bridge, sometimes right up through the floor.

He didn't tell his wife what he was doing. He only told her that Moor was giving him trouble over the payment for the bridge. He let her think that he was still working on the bridge. Mrs. Slater was a good woman, and Charlie knew she would be furious with him if she knew what was going on. Their farm was isolated, and they seldom had visitors, so it was several days before Mrs. Slater began to hear rumors.

As soon as she heard that something funny was going on at the Moortown bridge, she hitched up the farm wagon, put her two small children in the back, and drove to the bridge.

The wagon was well on its way across the bridge before Charlie, who had been dozing, woke up and grabbed his gun. He fired out to the side. He didn't want to shoot whoever was up there. He just didn't want them to cross the bridge.

When the gun boomed directly under its

belly, the horse reared and leaped sideways. Horse and wagon plunged through the side of the bridge and fell.

Mrs. Slater died, along with one of the children. The baby girl, Evelyn, was thrown clear and landed on a sandbar, unhurt.

For the next few years Charlie lived like a hermit with his little daughter. He never recovered from the shock of losing his wife and son and of being responsible for their deaths. Five years later he died himself.

Near the Moortown bridge.

It was his little daughter, Evvie, who found him.

Chapter 7

Pat and Curtis pulled their horses to a stop at the top of the hill and looked back down at Moortown. From here the bridge was hidden behind vine-hung trees. Only a corner of the deserted mill showed, bright cream in the sunlight.

"It happened a long time ago," Curtis said, as though trying to convince himself that the lingering unhappiness was now gone from the valley.

"I know," Pat said. "And yet our horses still wouldn't go across that bridge."

Curtis shrugged. "I heard somewhere that horses have an instinct about danger.

Maybe the wood in the bridge was more rotten than we thought, and it wouldn't have been strong enough to hold the horses' weight. Maybe they could sense that somehow, and that's why they didn't go across."

Pat was quiet for a long time. "Maybe," she said softly. "And maybe not."

About the Author

Lynn Hall has written more than twenty-five books for young readers. Because she has always loved dogs and horses and they fill a big portion of her life, many of her books are about them. Even when she is not specifically writing about dogs or horses, these favorite animals often sneak into her stories and play at least minor roles.

In recent years Ms. Hall has realized a lifelong dream with the completion of Touchwood, a small stone cottage planted squarely in the middle of twenty-five acres of woods and hills in northeast Iowa. "I designed the house myself," she writes, "and have had a hand in all phases of its construction, doing all but the heavy work myself, so it is a home in all the best senses of the word."

At Touchwood Ms. Hall also has built a kennel and small stable. There she raises English cocker spaniels and Paso Fino horses, which she breeds and shows in competition throughout the country.